W9-AQD-399
squishy #2
Fig. 1
cool!
WILDWOOD ELEMENTARY
#1 worry detective
#1

STOP
TODAY
first day of school!

HATTIE HARMONY
worry detective
Detective is IN
By ELIZABETH OLSEN
& ROBBIE ARNETT
Illustrated by
MARISSA VALDEZ
VIKING
5 yrs
4
3 yrs
2 yRS

THE FIRST DAY OF SCHOOL had finally arrived!

Some kids were excited AND a little worried.

Luckily, Wildwood Elementary had Hattie Harmony, Worry Detective.

Hattie had many tools up her sleeve, and she was ready to get to WORK!

emotions
There
Hattie Harmony, Worry Detective. How can I help solve your worries today?

“Hattie, it’s Pearl Peppercorn. I’m terribly worried about my first day of school. I have nervous butterflies flying all around my belly. What if no one plays with me at recess? What if I don’t make any new friends?”

Hattie put on her trusty Worry Detective Tool Belt. “Don’t you worry,” she said. “Meet me at the flagpole in front of school. I’ll be there just as soon as you can say . . .”

WORRY, WORRY, GO AWAY! There's no time for you today!
HH

It sounded like a case of the first day JITTERS.

As soon as she saw Pearl, Hattie pulled out two big nets.

Hattie gave one net to Pearl and kept the other for herself.

Pearl was confused.

"The butterflies aren't outside," Pearl said. "They're *inside* my belly."

But Hattie was already swinging her net.

WHOOOSH!
WHOOOSH!
WHOOSH!

The butterflies danced with the birds, boogied with the bees, slept in the grass, and even climbed up the trees.

Pearl and Hattie were having so much fun catching and releasing the butterflies that suddenly Pearl realized . . .

"Wait a minute," Pearl said as she rubbed her belly. "I don't feel the butterflies anymore! HOORAY!"

"That's right," said Hattie. "If we focus on our movement and try to LIVE IN THE MOMENT, our worries can fly away."

With Hattie's help, Pearl was now ready to start her first day of school.

"Thank you, Hattie Harmony," Pearl said.

The school bell rang.

Just as soon as Hattie sat down at her table, her friend Seymour Swiggletooth scooted right next to her.

"Psst, Hattie. I don't know what I'll do if Mrs. Rivers calls on me," whispered Seymour. "What if I don't know the answer? What if I have to stand up in front of the whole entire class? Ooooh, Hattie, my legs feel like Jell-O."

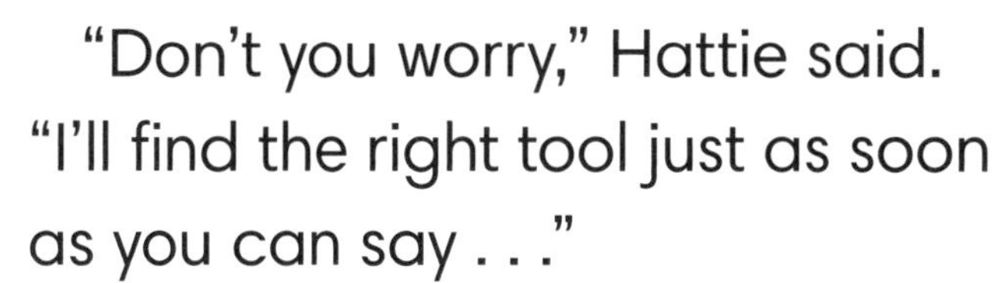

"Don't you worry," Hattie said. "I'll find the right tool just as soon as you can say . . ."

Hattie searched her trusty Worry Detective Tool Belt.
"AHA!" She knew just what she needed to solve this case.

In a flash, she pulled out one of her favorite tools:

SQUISHY BALL!

“What?! This is an emergency,” Seymour squealed. “I don’t have any time to play with a ball.”

“Oh, but this ball is special,” said Hattie. “Go ahead, give it a squeeze.”

Seymour squeezed
and he squeezed
and he squeezed.

"It's working!"
Seymour cheered.
"I don't feel so tense.
But how did you do it?"

"You did it!" Hattie said.
"By tensing other muscles
and squeezing Squishy Ball,
you told your worried mind
to relax and take a break."

“Thank you, Hattie. Now I’m ready to raise my hand in class!” said Seymour. “Can I keep it?”

“It’s yours!” Hattie said.

Recess was finally here!

Hattie and Pearl played one of their favorite games: TAG!

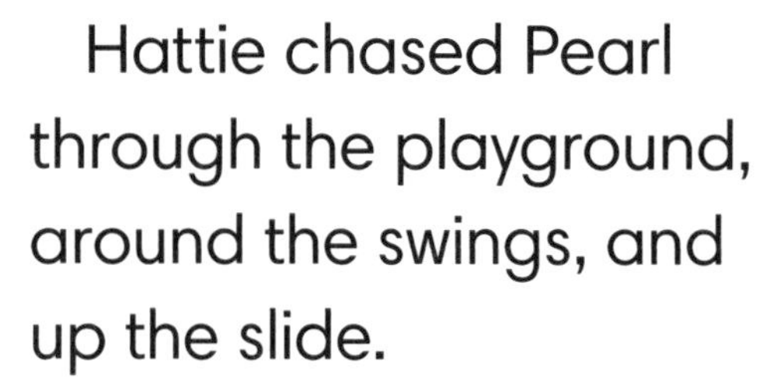

Hattie chased Pearl through the playground, around the swings, and up the slide.

"Come and get me!" Pearl shouted. But Hattie was worried.

She had never climbed to the top of the big slide before.

"What if I slide too fast, or what if I fall off? What if I don't like it?" Hattie asked.

"Hattie, you're the bravest person I know. You can do anything!"

"Brave people don't always feel brave inside," Hattie whispered. "I feel scared."

Hattie searched her Tool Belt.
In a flash, she pulled out MISS MIRROR.
Hattie saw fear in her eyes. But then she smiled and said to herself, "I am scared, but . . ."

I can do it!

cool!
YOU got this!
Miss Mirror

WORRY, WORRY, GO AWAY! THERE'S NO TIME FOR YOU TODAY!
WHOOSH

"Hattie, you did it!" Pearl cheered. "You conquered your fear!"

Even Hattie sometimes needed a reminder that having courage means facing our fears and pushing through them.

The first day of school had come to an end.

Duncan Delmar panicked as all the buses arrived at the pickup zone.

There were so many!

A BUS OVER HERE.

A BUS OVER THERE.

A BUS OVER THERE.

HELP!

“I can’t remember which is mine. My heart is racing! How will I ever get home?” said Duncan.

"Don't worry," said Hattie. "We'll find your bus just as soon as you can say . . ."

WORRY, WORRY,

GO AWAY!

Hattie searched through her trusty Worry Detective Tool Belt.

THERE'S NO
TIME FOR
YOU TODAY!

She searched and searched, but then she realized, "We don't need anything from my Tool Belt. We already have everything we need."

"We do?" asked Duncan.

"You bet we do. One of our greatest tools is something we do all the time without even thinking about it . . . WE BREATHE."

Hattie shut her eyes and slowly breathed in through her nose . . .

1-2-3

And slowly breathed out through her mouth . . .

1-2-3-4

"Now you try," Hattie said to Duncan.

Duncan breathed in . . .

1-2-3

Duncan breathed out . . .

1-2-3-4

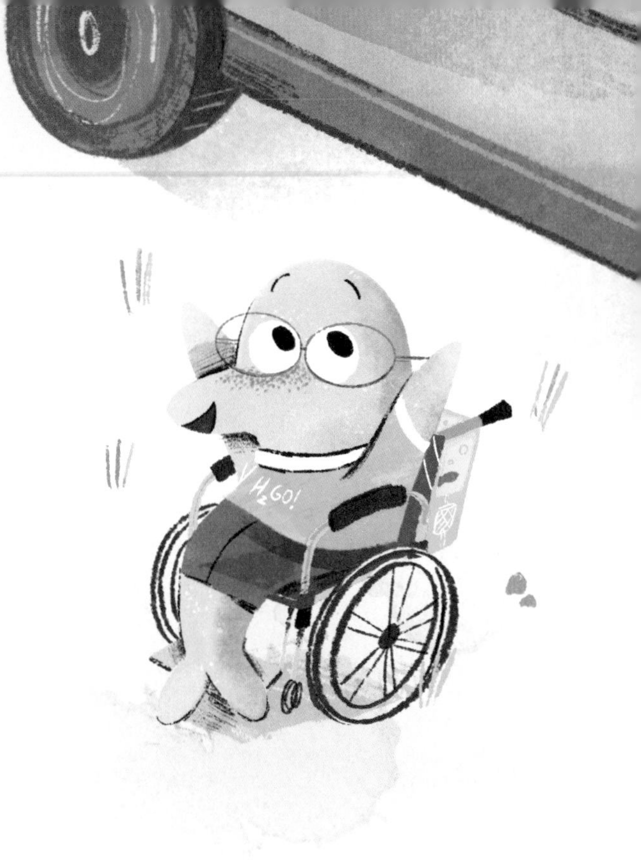

“Wow, those breaths made my heart slow down! I can think more clearly now,” said Duncan. “And look, there’s my bus!”

“When we take a moment to breathe in and breathe out, we can slow down all of the racing thoughts in our mind,” Hattie said.

"The first day of school was a blast!" Pearl exclaimed.
"We learned so much," Hattie said.

"Sometimes our worries can seem BIGGER than they really are. But as long as we remember that our minds are very, very powerful, and now that we have the tools to practice, we can conquer anything!

"Oh, and one more thing." Hattie smiled. "If you ever need me, you can always call your friend . . ."

Hattie Harmony,
Worry Detective.
Belongs to H.H.

AUTHORS' NOTE

Look all around you. Everyone you see is filled with feelings and emotions—from happy to sad, courageous to fearful, and so many more. Learning how to identify your feelings is the first step to becoming aware of all your emotions, big and small. Everyone needs a little help when it comes to managing emotions like anxiety, so that's why Hattie Harmony uses the tools below and empowering self-talk to soothe many kinds of worries.

As two people who deeply believe in the importance of mindful thinking, we hope the Hattie Harmony series will inspire children to be curious, empathetic, and resilient in an anxious world that has many unknown challenges.

TOOLS USED IN THIS BOOK:

MINDFUL MOVEMENT: Focused movement of our bodies can help the spinning thoughts in our heads slow down. This movement returns our minds to the present moment instead of worrying about the future. This is how Hattie helps Pearl Peppercorn with the butterfly nets.

STRESS BALLS: Stress balls are a tool you can use to signal to the brain that everything is okay. When we squeeze a stress ball, the physical tension of squeezing and releasing our muscles allows the rest of the body to relax, relieving tension caused by stress. This is how Hattie helps Seymour Swiggletooth with the squishy ball. Don't have a squishy ball? No problem. You can tense your muscles and release them for the same positive effect.

FACING YOUR FEAR: The acknowledgment of fear is encouraged in cognitive behavioral therapy because it teaches a child to tolerate their anxiety instead of being controlled by it. Avoiding our fears is only a short-term solution that can lead to other compulsive behaviors. Hattie uses a mirror meditation in order to face her own fear. By seeing her facial expressions in the mirror, she can recognize her emotions and start to manage them. This meditation can also help us be in the moment or build confidence by using positive self-talk.

MINDFUL BREATHING: Mindful breathing is another way to relax. When we exhale longer than we inhale, we send a signal to our brain to turn on our parasympathetic nervous system, which commands our rest-and-digest mode. This can lower cortisol levels and our heart rate for a calmer body. Hattie uses a breathing exercise to help Duncan Delmar.

For Dottie, Ruby, Rafi, Lucy, Zoe, Mable, Hart, and Henry
—E. O. and R. A.

For Kelly, the best worry detective/agent I could've asked for
—M. V.

VIKING
An imprint of Penguin Random House LLC, New York

First published in the United States of America by Viking,
an imprint of Penguin Random House LLC, 2022

Visit us online at penguinrandomhouse.com.

Library of Congress Cataloging-in-Publication Data is available.

Printed in the United States of America

ISBN 9780593351444

10 9 8 7 6 5 4 3 2 1

PC

Book design by Marissa Valdez and Jim Hoover Set in Harmonia Sans Pro

The authors wish to thank Mrs. Suzie S. Foger and Dr. Donna DeFazio, LCSW

squishy #2
hello?
fig. 1
WILDWOOD ELEMENTARY
COOL!
#1 worry
#1
detective!

You got this!
cool!
Miss Mirror
TODAY
school!
squishy #1
breathe!